SIMON
PHILIP

MAGDA
BROL

# ESME
## AND THE SABRE-TOOTHED CUB

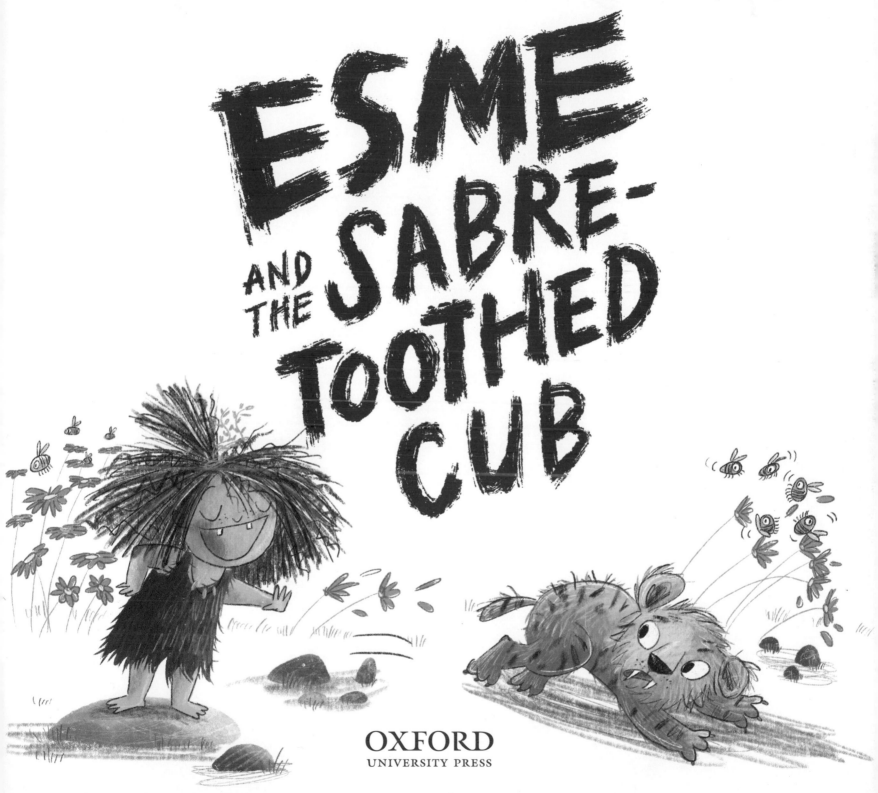

**OXFORD**
UNIVERSITY PRESS

Once upon a very, **very** long time ago, when there was **nothing** on TV, a stranger strolled into the village.

'Look, Morris!' Esme said to her best friend. 'He's so cute!'

The other kids thought so, too.

But the adults could only see the dangerous
creature the cub would become.

'SHOOOO!' they shouted. 'GO AWAY!'

And luckily, he did.

But the very next day . . .

and the day after that . . .

and the day after *that* . . .

he came back, despite the adults' shouts.

Esme knew that the cub loved
the food she left out.

'Would you like to be my
pet?' she asked. She'd always
wanted a pet of her own.

The cub said nothing.

'Great!' Esme said.
'Let's call him Seb!'

But Morris wasn't sure that Seb
wanted to be *anyone's* pet . . .

. . . as Esme would soon find out.

SIT!

STAY!

In fact, the harder Esme tried to make Seb her pet . . .

. . . the harder things became.

'Nothing's working, Morris!' Esme moaned.
'Seb *doesn't* want to be my pet!'

Morris had known that all
along. But *he* knew what
would work . . .

The next day, Morris decided to make friends with Seb.
Esme wanted to join in too, but she still felt too cross.

Morris and Seb played, *together* . . .

They hid, *together* . . .

They lay down,
*together* . . .

When they went for a walk,
Esme followed them at
a distance.

But there was
trouble ahead.

Luckily, Esme knew **exactly** what to do. Using her *very* **loudest** voice, she bellowed,

'Now I get it!'
Esme said.

'Seb's not my pet—
he's our friend!'

From then on, Esme, Morris and Seb had fun *together*.

And though Esme loved playing, just the three of them . . .

. . . she knew that all the other kids would **LOVE** playing with Seb, too!

# OXFORD
## UNIVERSITY PRESS

Great Clarendon Street, Oxford OX2 6DP
Oxford University Press is a department of the University of Oxford.
It furthers the University's objective of excellence in research, scholarship,
and education by publishing worldwide. Oxford is a registered trade mark of
Oxford University Press in the UK and in certain other countries

British Library Cataloguing in Publication Data

Data available
ISBN: 978-0-19-277504-7

1 3 5 7 9 10 8 6 4 2

Printed in China

Paper used in the production of this book is a natural,
recyclable product made from wood grown in sustainable forests.
The manufacturing process conforms to the environmental
regulations of the country of origin.

# COIN CATCHER

**Pile the coins and flip them all,
then catch them quick: don't let them fall!**

You will need:
.....................
- about 10 coins of the same value

**Difficulty:** ⭐⭐⭐⭐⭐ **Players:** any number

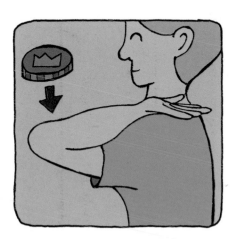

**1** Bend your arm back so that your hand rests on top of your shoulder, as in the picture.

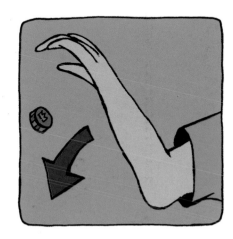

**2** Place a coin on the flat part of your elbow. Now jerk your arm down so the coin flies off – can you catch it in mid-air with the hand of that arm?

**3** When you can catch one coin, try again with two or more coins in a pile.

The winner is... the person who can catch the biggest tower of coins.

**Bet You Can't!** Catch more than ten coins in a pile!

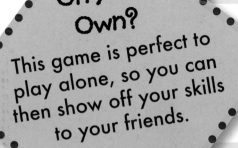

**On Your Own?** This game is perfect to play alone, so you can then show off your skills to your friends.

# JACKS

Pick up jacks and catch the ball,
see if you can scoop them all.

**Difficulty:** ⭐⭐⭐⭐ **Players:** any number

**You will need:**
...................
- set of jacks or some pebbles
- small bouncy ball

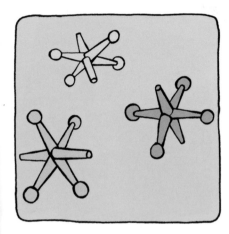

**1** Set out your jacks or pebbles in a row. It is easiest to play on a hard floor or a table.

**2** Bounce your ball, gently, and while it is in the air, scoop up one jack. Use the hand holding the jack to catch the ball after it bounces a second time.

**3** Now do it again scooping up two jacks, then three, then four…

**On Your Own?**
No problem – this game was designed to play alone.

**The winner is...** the person who can scoop up the most jacks and still catch the ball.

**Bet You Can't!** Catch the ball before it bounces a second time!

31

# HIDE AND SNAP

Memory's good and eyes are keen?
Try to remember what you've seen.

**Difficulty:** ⭐⭐⭐⭐ **Players:** 2 equal teams

**You will need:**
.............
- 2 packs of cards

**1** Before you play, someone hides the cards from one pack, individually, around the house. You could hide them in bookshelves, or in the fridge, or under furniture.

**2** This player then hands out cards from the other pack to all team members. They have to find the matching card and return it to the 'hider' to score a point. They are then given another card to match.

**3** Compare cards with your team mates to help them find theirs, too.

*The winner is...* the team with the most points after a set time.

**Bet You Can't!**
Remember which cards you have seen, so you can find the pairs more quickly.

**On Your Own?**
Hide the cards yourself, face down, then play the game to match them all up.

30

# WHERE IN THE WORLD?

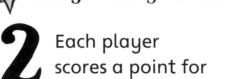

Rack your brains for all you're worth, to work your way around the Earth.

**Difficulty:** ★★★★ **Players:** any number

**2** Each player scores a point for knowing about their chosen country: which continent it is on, its capital city and the main language spoken. Use the map or an atlas to check the answers.

**3** Score extra points for additional facts, such as currency, famous places or famous people from your country.

**You will need:**
..................
• map of the world
• pencil

**1** Open up the map and take turns to close your eyes and pick a place with the pencil.

## On Your Own?
This is still fun – pick places at random and test your own knowledge.

## The winner is...
everyone – it's better to play just for fun as it's easier to answer questions about some countries than others.

## Did You Know?
The biggest country in the world is Russia, but the country with the most people is China.

29

# CARD LOTTERY

"Higher! Lower!" you must shout,
but two the same will catch you out!

**Difficulty:** ⭐⭐⭐ **Players:** any number

**You will need:**
.................
• pack of cards

**3** Player one keeps going until they get one wrong. The turned-over cards are theirs to keep. The next player now has a turn. If the next card is the same number, you are also out.

**1** Shuffle the cards, then turn over the top one onto your playing surface.

**2** Player one has to say if the next card is going to be higher or lower than the one showing. That's easy if it's a King, but harder if it's a middle card such as a seven.

### Did You Know?

This game used to be a TV show called *Play Your Cards Right*.

The winner is...
the person holding the most cards after three turns each.

### On Your Own?

You can still play, guessing 'higher' or 'lower' before you turn each card.

# BASKETBALL

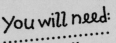

**You will need:**
...............
- soft ball
- wastepaper basket

Who can throw their ball the best? This game will put you to the test.

**Difficulty:** ⭐⭐⭐ **Players:** any number

**1** Place a wastepaper basket on one side of the room. Take four steps backwards.

**3** You are allowed three goes to get it in. If you miss, you are out. If you are successful, you go through to the next round, where you have to take an extra step backwards.

## Did You Know?

When 'real' basketball was invented, they used peach-collecting baskets – so this game is pretty similar!

**2** The idea is to score a 'basket' by throwing or bouncing the ball into the bin.

The winner is...
the person who qualifies for the most rounds.

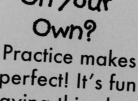

On Your Own?
Practice makes perfect! It's fun playing this alone.

# PEA BRAINS

**Suck really hard to move those peas, try not to spill them, if you please!**

**Difficulty:** ⭐⭐⭐   **Players:** any number

**3** Stop when all the peas have been sucked up. Ignore any that have dropped on the floor – yuck!

**1** Each player needs an empty bowl and a drinking straw. Place a bowl of peas (or chocolate chips – even better!) between the players.

**2** Each player tries to suck a pea onto the end of their straw, then move it across to their own bowl. Everyone plays at once!

The winner is... the player with the most peas in their bowl.

## Did You Know?

In the United States you can buy a drink that is 'green pea' flavoured – now that's easy to suck up with your straw!

## On Your Own?

See how many peas you can move in one minute.

26

# DICE GOLF

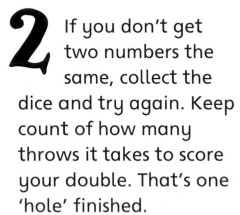

It's hard to score a hole in one, but trying gives you lots of fun.

**Difficulty:** ⭐⭐⭐ **Players:** any number

**2** If you don't get two numbers the same, collect the dice and try again. Keep count of how many throws it takes to score your double. That's one 'hole' finished.

**3** Let each player have their turn at throwing. Everyone needs to get 18 doubles, like the 18 holes of a golf course. Keep track of all the scores.

**1** On your turn, throw the three dice together. You are trying to get a double – for example, two fives.

The winner is... the person with the lowest score after 18 holes.

## On Your Own?
Play just the same, and keep a record of your best scores.

## Bet You Can't!
Score a hole in one – a double on your first throw!

# RUNNY NOSES

Drop a card below your nose,
fingers crossed for where it goes!

**You will need:**
........................
- pack of cards
- 2 buckets

**Difficulty:** ⭐ ⭐ ⭐   **Players:** 2 equal teams

**1** Each team stands by their bucket. Team one has the red cards and team two has the black cards.

**2** Player one must take a card and hold it so that the short edge touches the bottom of their nose, pointing downwards. They let go of the card to see if it falls into the bucket.

**3** Player one tries with all their team's cards. Pick up any that have missed the bucket, and let player two try with those, and so on.

The winner is... the first team to get all 26 cards in their bucket.

## Did You Know?
Before cards had hearts, diamonds, clubs and spades on them, the pictures were coins, cups, swords and sticks.

## On Your Own?
Practise on your own – it's harder than it sounds!

24

# ON YOUR MARKS

You will need:
...............
• various items listed in steps 2 and 3

**Racing games will keep you busy, be careful that you don't get dizzy!**

**Difficulty:** ⭐ ⭐  **Players:** any number

**1** You can play racing games indoors as well as outdoors, as long as you play carefully. Use items that will not break anything. Look at steps 2 and 3 for ideas.

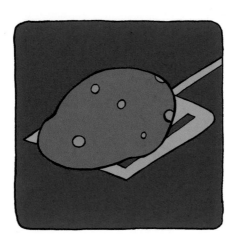

**Bet You Can't!**
Wriggle along on your bottom while carrying a marble with your toes.

**2** Have an egg and spoon race but using a feather in a bowl, or carrying a potato on a fish slice. Both are tricky!

**3** Give each player a newspaper that they must use to flap a piece of paper across the room. Try crawling along the floor while pushing a ball along with your nose, or holding a balloon between your knees.

**On Your Own?**
Make up your own wacky races, or try to set new solo record times.

The winner is... the first to finish, obviously!

# TOTALLY

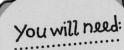

Throw high numbers if you're able,
add the three dice on the table.

**Difficulty:**  **Players:** 2 or more

You will need:
- pencils
- paper
- 3 dice

**1** The first player throws all three dice. Take out the dice with the highest number, then throw the other two.

**2** Take out the dice with the highest number again, then throw the last dice.

**3** Add up the score from all three of your dice. Now let the next player have a turn.

The winner is... the person with the highest score.

## Bet You Can't!
Put a counter in the middle for each player. The winner of each round wins all the counters. If there is a draw, leave the winnings as a 'rollover'.

## On Your Own?
Play just the same, trying to beat your own highest score.

22

# MOUNTAIN CLIMBING

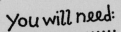

**Try to throw right every time, the number mountain's hard to climb!**

**Difficulty:** ⭐⭐ **Players:** any number

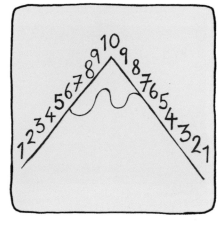

**1** Each player writes down the numbers 1 to 10 and back to 1 again, as shown here.

**2** Take turns to throw the two dice. Anyone who gets a 1 crosses it off their list. If you are lucky and get a 2 as well, cross that off, too.

**3** Keep throwing the dice and crossing off the numbers, in order. To cross out the bigger numbers, add the two numbers on the dice together. For example, if your throw is a 3 and a 4, you can cross off seven (3 + 4 = 7).

**Bet You Can't!**
Play with numbers 1 to 12, and cross off the highest ones first.

**On Your Own?**
See how many turns it takes you to reach the end, and compare your best scores.

**The winner is...** the first person to climb their 'mountain' of numbers and get back down the other side.

21

# BEETLEDICE

You need to shake a six to start, then draw each beetle body part.

**Difficulty:**  **Players:** 2 or more

**1** Take turns to throw the dice, and try to draw a whole beetle. The number you throw tells you which part of the beetle you can draw.

**2**
6 = body
5 = head
4 = leg
3 = eye
2 = antenna
1 = mouth

**3** You can only draw a leg or a head if you have already drawn a body, so you must throw a six first. You may not add eyes, antennae or a mouth until you have drawn the head.

## On Your Own?

Draw two different coloured beetles, taking turns to throw the dice for each one, and see which one wins.

## Did You Know?

There are more different types of beetle than of any other kind of insect. Maybe your picture is another new species!

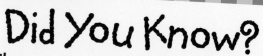

The winner is...
the first person to finish drawing their beetle with all its parts including six legs.

20

# SNAP!

You will need:
- pack of cards

Here's a game you'll like to play,
it's brilliant for a rainy day.

**Difficulty:** ⭐⭐ **Players:** 2

**1** Divide the pack in half, so each player has 26 cards. Hold them facing downwards, so you can only see the backs.

**2** Take turns to play one card each onto a pile in the middle.

**3** If you see a card that is the same number or picture as the one before it, shout "Snap!" If you shout first, you pick up the whole pile. Now carry on as before.

## On Your Own?
Play really quickly, turning over cards with both hands. Can you still spot the 'Snaps' at top speed?

## The winner is...
the person with the most cards, or with the whole pack if you play to the end.

19

# SARDINES

This game's great to play inside, find somewhere cool where you can hide.

**Difficulty:** ⭐⭐ **Players:** 4 or more

**You will need:**
• permission to hide in different rooms

**1** One player finds a hiding place, while the other players close their eyes and count to 100.

**2** The players split up and try to find the hider. If you find them, join them in their hiding place and keep very quiet.

## On Your Own?

Draw a map of your house, and mark with an 'X' all the good hiding places you know.

**3** Play carries on until the last player finds all the others squeezed in together, under a bed or inside a large airing cupboard!

## Did You Know?

This game's name comes from tins of small fish called sardines. Lots of sardines are packed tightly into a small space.

The winner is...
no one, but the last finder becomes the next hider.

18

# TREASURE HUNT

**Ten things to find from store and shelf, can you collect them by yourself?**

**Difficulty:** ⭐⭐ **Players:** any number

**You will need:**
................
- plastic container
- pencils
- paper

**3** Some things to find: teaspoon, coaster, story book, fruit, paper clip, clothes peg, sock, toy car, yellow pen, photograph.

**1** Each player needs a list of items to find. Use the ideas in step 3, or make up your own. If the players are very young, draw pictures instead.

**2** Use your plastic container to collect your items in. It's a race to see who can get all ten items first.

The winner is... the first person to collect all ten things on their list.

## On Your Own?

Use the list in step 3 and see how fast you can find them all.

## Did You Know?

In the UK, 'treasure' such as buried coins only counts as official treasure if it is more than 300 years old – so nothing on this list really counts!

17

# SINGING STAR

You will need:
...............
• music, from CDs or an MP3 player

Out of tune or singing fine,
see if you can keep in time.

**Difficulty:** ⭐⭐ **Players:** any number

**1** Take turns to choose a favourite song. Start it playing until it gets to the chorus.

**2** Just as the chorus starts, turn down the volume. You have to carry on singing.

**3** When you have sung the chorus, turn the music up again. Have you kept in time with the singers?

The winner is...
no one, but some people are much better at this than others.

### On Your Own?

No problem – sing all your favourite songs and see how good you are at keeping time.

### Bet You Can't!

Turn down the volume during a verse, not the chorus – and try not to forget the words!

# CARD WARS

Lay your cards – 1, 2, 3, 4,
the winner must get rid of more.

**Difficulty:**  **Players:** 2 or more (4 or 5 is best)

**1** Deal out the cards to the players. It's OK if some players have one more card than others.

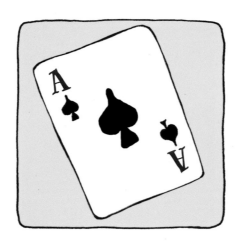

**2** The player to the left of the dealer puts her lowest card on the table. Let's say it is the four of hearts. The player with the five of hearts then plays that card, and so on, up to the King of hearts.

**3** Whoever played the King then starts the game again, by placing his lowest card.

The winner is... the first person to get rid of all their cards.

## Did You Know?

During the Second World War, playing cards helped US soldiers in prisoner of war camps. Special cards were sent to them containing maps of the area, so they could plan their escape.

## On Your Own?

Lay the four Aces on the table, then turn over the cards looking for twos, then threes and so on. How many times do you have to work through the pack to complete the four suits?

15

# SOCKEY

Your room is much too small for hockey, so why not try this game of sockey?!

**Difficulty:** ⭐⭐  **Players:** 2 equal teams

**2** One person is the caller and knows what is in each sock. They shout out an item for the teams to bring them.

**1** Each team has a long sock filled with small items such as toys, wrapped sweets, marbles and coins.

### Bet You Can't!
Make the game more tricky by putting two large things in the sock that get in the way, such as an apple and a potato.

**3** A team can only pull out one item at a time, so if you are trying to find a red marble it's frustrating if you keep pulling out a blue one! Score a point if your team hands over the item first.

### On Your Own?
Fill a sock and see how fast you can find matching pairs, for example two golden sweets or two pennies.

### The winner is...
the team with the most points at the end.

14

# PICTURE PUZZLE

In your picture what do you see? how many things start with 't'?

**Difficulty:**  **Players:** any number

You will need:
....................
- magazines or travel guides
- pens

**2** Each player is given a picture and a letter of the alphabet. Choose common letters such as 's', 'p' or 't'.

**1** Look in magazines for pictures with lots of things in them. Pictures of people at the beach, shopping or at a theme park are good choices.

### On Your Own?
This is a great way to pass some time alone.

**3** Draw a circle around all the items in your picture that begin with your letter.

## Did You Know?
More English words begin with 's' or 't' than with any other letter of the alphabet.

## The winner is...
no one, as some pictures might just have more things in them than others.

13

# DRESSING UP

**Grab your clothes and put them on, this racing game is fashion fun!**

**Difficulty:**  **Players:** 2 equal teams

**3** Each player in the team takes their turn to grab the bag and get dressed and undressed.

**1** Each team has a bag of clothes. They can be funny holiday clothes, such as a floppy hat, flip-flops and a patterned shirt, or any other dressing-up outfits. Put them on a chair.

**2** Play as a relay race. Player one runs to the chair, puts on all the clothes, runs once around the chair, takes off the clothes and repacks the bag, then runs back to the start.

The winner is... the first team to finish.

## On Your Own?
Beat the clock – can you complete the course in less than two minutes?

## Did You Know?
Flip-flops were worn in Ancient Egypt by important people, and they can be seen in their wall paintings.

# JACK OF THE PACK

Jack of hearts, or clubs, or spades –
who'll have most cards when you've played?

**Difficulty:** ★ **Players:** up to 4

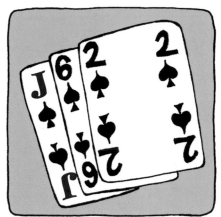

**3** Keep taking turns until all the cards are used up.

**The winner is...**
the player whose Jack has the most cards next to it by the end of the pack.

**1** Separate the Jacks from the pack of cards. Each player chooses one. Place all the Jacks in the centre of the table, face up. Place the rest of the pack face down next to them.

**2** Take turns to turn over the top card from the pack. If it matches the suit of your Jack, put it next to him, overlapping slightly. If it does not match, it goes into a throwaway pile.

## Did You Know?
In playing cards, the Jack used to be called the Knave. The card had 'Kn' on it instead of 'J', with the picture.

## On Your Own?
Play with two Jacks, one red and one black, to see which one wins.

11

# BLOWOUT

**For this game you'll need lots of puff, but can your team blow hard enough?**

**Difficulty:**  **Players:** any number

**1** Play this game if you are not allowed to play football indoors. You can play on a table, or on the floor.

**2** Set up a goal at each end of the 'pitch'. You could use blocks or modelling clay as markers.

**3** The idea is to score a goal against your opponents. You move the ball around by blowing on it through your straw. Your straw cannot touch the ball!

### On Your Own?
Make an obstacle course using blocks and toys to blow your ball around.

### Bet You Can't!
Add extra 'players' onto the pitch, such as stones or toys, to act as defenders.

The winner is... the first person to score three goals.

# MATCHING PAIRS

Hide a sock behind the telly,
you'll find it fast if it's too smelly!

**Difficulty:**  **Players:** 2 or more

**1** Gather together lots of pairs of things. Hide one of each pair around the house.

**2** Each player is given the other one of a pair, and has to try to find the matching object.

**3** It's no use finding a red glove if you're looking for a blue one – you have to find an exact match.

## Did You Know?

It could take ages to play this with Joshua Meller of the United States – he owns more than 600 pairs of Converse shoes!

## The winner is...
the first person to find their matching pair.

## On Your Own?

Find things that go together – it could be items such as a bat and a ball, or a spoon and a fork.

9

# PENNIES IN THE POT

**You will need:**
..........
- 10 counters or coins per player
- 3 dice
- pot or cup

Put your pennies in the pot, see if you can spend the lot!

**Difficulty:** ⭐ **Players:** 2 or more

**1** Each player chooses a number from one to six. If two people are playing, they choose three numbers each. If there are three players, each one chooses two numbers.

**3** So, if 1-5-5 is thrown, the player who chose one pays one coin, and the player who chose five pays two coins.

**2** Take turns to throw the three dice together. If your number shows, you can put a counter or a coin in the pot.

*The winner is...* the first person to get all their coins in the pot.

### On Your Own?
Choose a number and see how many times you have to throw the dice to get all your coins in the pot.

## Did You Know?
This game is also called 'Help your Neighbour', because you are likely to throw their numbers and help them get rid of their coins.

8

# WORKS OF ART

Draw yourself – we think you'll find it's not so easy drawing blind!

**Difficulty:**  **Players:** any number

You will need:
- scarves
- pencils
- paper

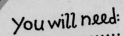

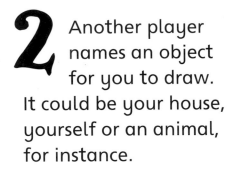

**2** Another player names an object for you to draw. It could be your house, yourself or an animal, for instance.

**1** Use a scarf for a blindfold – or just close your eyes, but do not cheat!

**3** You must then draw that object without peeping at your paper. When you take a look, you'll laugh at what you've drawn!

**On Your Own?**
Challenge yourself to draw something – no peeping!

**Bet You Can't!**
Name something the item MUST have, such as the right number of windows on the house.

The winner is...
no one, this game is just for fun.

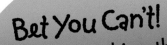

# DINOSAUR HUNT

Hide T. Rex or brontosaurus,
they'll say, "D'you think he saw us?"

**Difficulty:** ⭐ **Players:** 2 or more

**1** One player hides the dinosaur in a room away from the other players.

**2** Hide it somewhere tricky to find, but not impossible. It could be on a bookshelf, or by the TV. Don't hide it in the laundry basket – it will never be found!

**3** The other players come in and search the room, trying to find the dinosaur.

The winner is... the person who finds the dinosaur – they can take the next turn to hide it.

## On Your Own?

Close your eyes and spin around, then throw the dinosaur. Spin again and open your eyes to start searching.

## Did You Know?

In olden times this game was called 'Hunt the thimble'. A thimble is a small, cup-shaped item that fits over a finger – the perfect size for hiding.

6

# Difficulty

There is a large choice of games to put you to the test, whatever your skills or age. They are graded throughout the book, from * (easy peasy) to * * * * * (pretty tricky). Start near the beginning of the book, and challenge yourself as you move on to the harder games at the end.

## BLOWOUT

For this game you'll need lots of puff, but can your team blow hard enough?

**Difficulty:** ⭐ **Players:** any number

**1** Play this game if you are not allowed to play football indoors. You can play on a table, or on the floor.

**2** Set up a goal at each end of the 'pitch'. You could use blocks or modelling clay as markers.

**3** The idea is to score a goal against your opponents. You move the ball around by blowing on it through your straw. Your straw cannot touch the ball!

**You will need:**
- drinking straws
- small balls such as table tennis balls
- blocks or modelling clay

### On Your Own?
Make an obstacle course using blocks and toys to blow your ball around.

### Bet You Can't!
Add extra 'players' onto the pitch, such as stones or toys, to act as defenders.

**The winner is...** the first person to score three goals.

**10**

## JACK OF THE PACK

Jack of hearts, or clubs, or spades – who'll have most cards when you've played?

**Difficulty:** ⭐ **Players:** up to 4

**You will need:**
- pack of cards

**1** Separate the Jacks from the pack of cards. Each player chooses one. Place all the Jacks in the centre of the table, face up. Place the rest of the pack face down next to them.

**2** Take turns to turn over the top card from the pack. If it matches the suit of your Jack, put it next to him, overlapping slightly. If it does not match, it goes into a throwaway pile.

**3** Keep taking turns until all the cards are used up.

**The winner is...** the player whose Jack has the most cards next to it by the end of the pack.

### On Your Own?
Play with two Jacks, one red and one black, to see which one wins.

### Did You Know?
In playing cards, the Jack used to be called the Knave. The card had 'Kn' on it instead of 'J', with the picture.

**11**

# Bet You Can't!

So, you've played the game a million times, and it's just too easy. Put yourself to the test by taking the 'Bet you can't' challenge, and see how smart you are then!

# Did You Know?

For some games you will find fascinating facts related to them, to add to the fun.

# HOW TO USE THIS BOOK

**It's raining, it's pouring, being at home is boring!**

What can you do if you are cooped up indoors, you have watched too much TV, finished your book and played enough computer games? Never fear – this book is full of games to play inside, without breaking anything or getting on anyone's nerves. You never know – you might be having so much fun that the grown-ups want to join in!

## You will need

The games are explained really simply, so you can read the instructions and play straight away. Some of them use everyday items that you can find around the house. You may need to grab a pen and paper to keep score, and a few of the games use dice or a pack of cards. Each game has a list of things you will need at the start, so you can be prepared.

## Players

Most of the games are for 2 or more players, to keep anyone who is bored out of mischief. If there is no one to play with you, read the 'On your own?' feature to see how to adapt the game and still have fun.

4

# CONTENTS